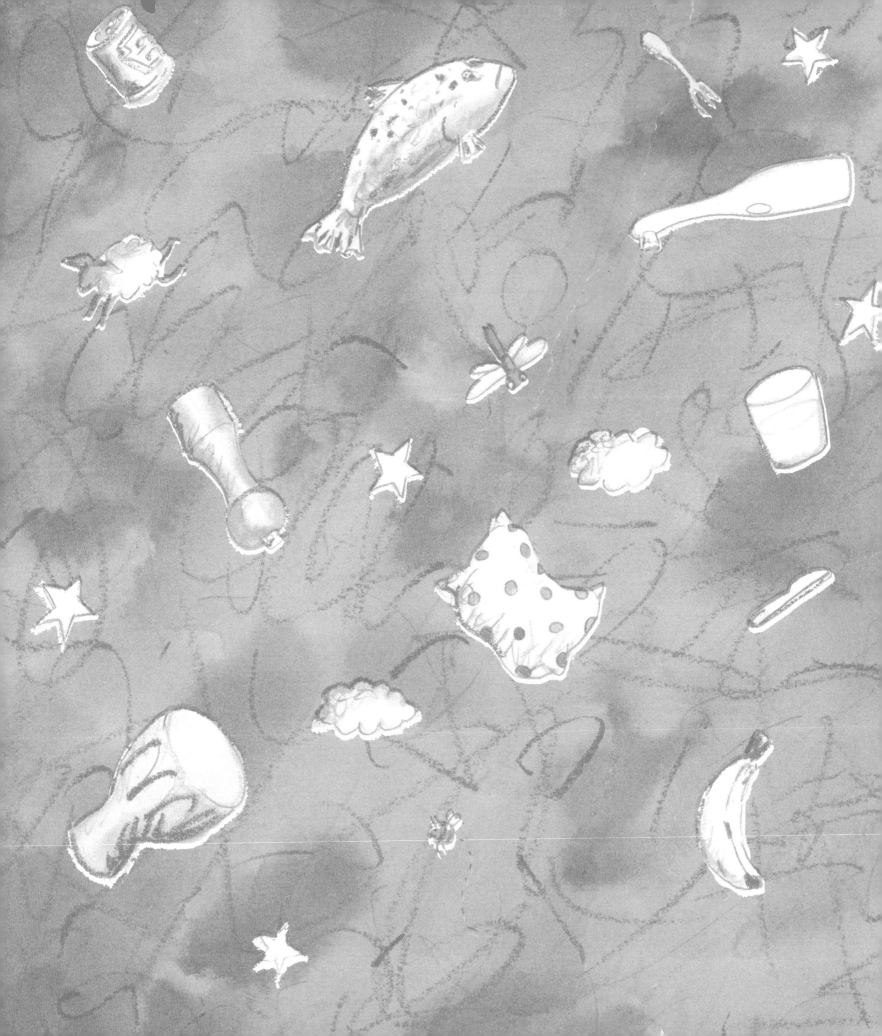

Never Ask a Dinosaur to Dinner

Written by Gareth Edwards
Illustrated by Guy Parker-Rees

Scholastic Press · New York

Never ask a dinosaur to dinner.
   Really, never ask a dinosaur to dinner.

   Because a T. rex is ferocious

   And his manners are atrocious,
   And you'll find that if he's able . . .

He will eat
the kitchen table!

He'll grow fatter while the rest of you grow thinner,
So never ask a dinosaur to dinner.

Please don't share your toothbrush with a shark.
Really, please don't share your
toothbrush with a shark.

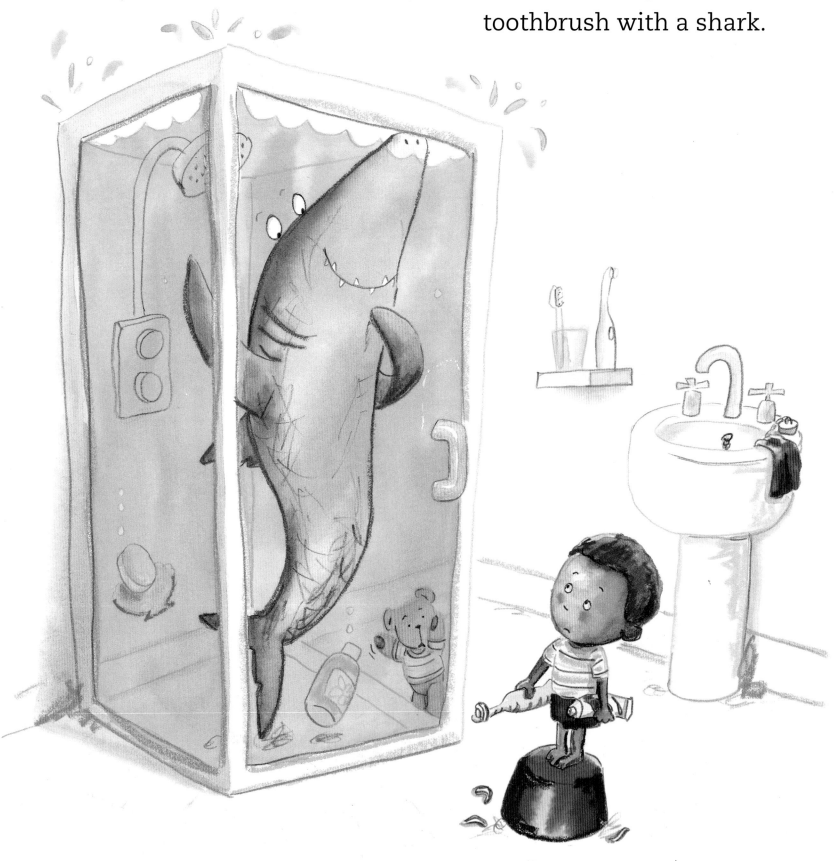

They've got so many rows of teeth
On the top and underneath,
And any self-respecting shark'll
Want each little tooth to sparkle.

If you rush him . . .

. . . he may make a rude remark,

So please don't share your toothbrush with a shark.

Never let a beaver in the sink.

Really, never let a beaver
in the sink.

He'll block it up
with sticks and mud,

And turn the taps
on till they flood,

And build a great big beaver dam, and
fill the whole thing up with salmon!

And the water won't be very
good to drink . . .

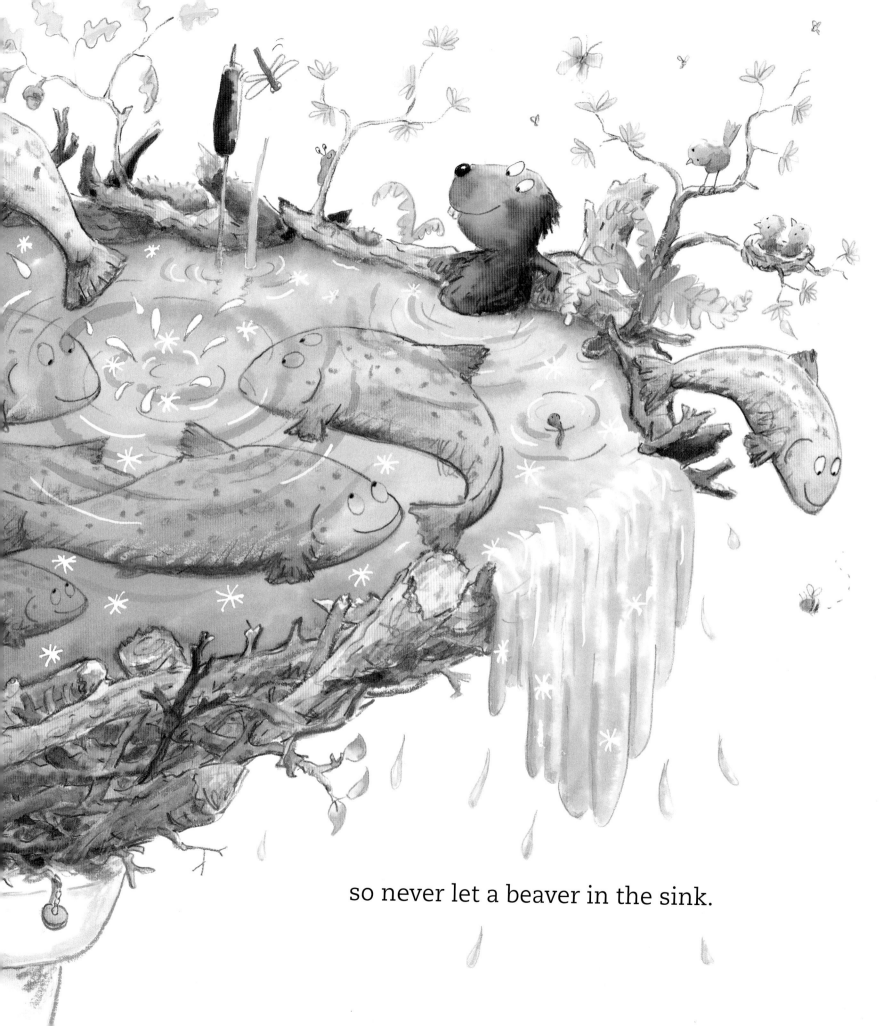

so never let a beaver in the sink.

Please don't use a tiger as a towel.

Really, please don't use
a tiger as a towel.

Because in case you have forgotten,
Tigers are not made of cotton,
And although they're furred quite thickly
They can get mad very quickly.

And you'll find they have
a rather scary growl,

So please don't use a tiger as a towel.

Never choose a bison for a blanket.

Really, never choose a bison for a blanket.

Because although it's warm and woolly,
You will find it is a bully,

And its hooves
will be too clumpy,

And its horns
will make you grumpy,

And by morning time
you will not want to thank it.

So never choose a bison for a blanket.

Please don't let
a barn owl in your bed.
Really, please don't let
a barn owl in your bed.

Because the first thing that you'll learn'll
Be a barn owl is nocturnal.
She will hunt for mice and hoot all night
And leave your bed a dreadful sight!

You'll wish that owl
was in a barn instead,

So please don't let a barn owl in your bed.

Now, here's how you can have a lovely sleep.
Really, here's how you can have a lovely sleep . . .

Say NO to beaver, shark, and owl!
Avoid the tiger and his growl!
Steer clear of every dinosaur!
Leave bison at the bedroom door!

These animals won't help you rest!

At bedtime here is what is best . . .

Stick to ONE teddy . . .

. . . and a flock of sheep.

And THAT'S how you can have a lovely sleep.

For my parents,
with love and
admiration – G.E.

Originally published in the UK in 2014 by Scholastic Children's Books

10 9 8 7 6 5 4 3   15 16 17 18 19

Printed in Malaysia   108
This edition first printing, May 2015

Library of Congress Cataloging-in-Publication Data

Edwards, Gareth, 1965- author.
Never ask a dinosaur to dinner / written by Gareth Edwards ; illustrated by Guy Parker-Rees. —
First US edition. pages cm "Originally published in the UK by Scholastic Children's Books."
Summary: Through a series of amusing examples, a young boy learns how to get ready for a good
night's sleep—and bedtime should not include dinosaurs or sharks.
ISBN 978-0-545-81296-2
1. Bedtime—Juvenile fiction. 2. Animals—Juvenile fiction. 3. Stories in rhyme. [1. Stories in
rhyme. 2. Bedtime—Fiction. 3. Animals—Fiction. 4. Humorous stories.] I. Parker-Rees, Guy,
illustrator. II. Title. PZ8.3.E266Ne 2015 [E]—dc23 2014030739

For Peter's
niece and nephew,
Allegra and Monty
– G.P-R.